## Contents

Written by ~~Emma~~

Illustrated by Helen Humphries

# Trouble

Boy, were we in a fix. Lost, hungry, cold, wet, and totally petrified. Oh, and did I mention trapped? I wasn't sure how we were going to get out of this mess, but it seemed everybody was looking to me for a solution. That's just the way it's always been. Don't worry, Max will know what to do. Max will fix it.

"Max, I'm hungry," said a small voice.

That was Tab, the smallest in our gang and quite possibly the biggest eater. Always eating, that one. I don't know where she puts it as she's scrawny as anything. Hollow legs, Joanie reckons. It was over an hour since we had eaten so I wasn't surprised she was feeling a little hungry. She usually only goes ten minutes without stuffing something into her mouth. If we didn't get out soon, we would starve to death. And that wasn't a prospect I was looking forward to. I didn't mind the starving bit so much, I was used to going without food. It was Tab's whining about it that I didn't think I could stand.

Let me fill you in so you can begin to understand the predicament we were in – "we" being me, Billy, Tab, Toby, and Reggie.

I'm Max, the oldest of the Bunton kids. Billy and Tab are my younger brother and sister respectively. Our dad's somewhere else. I'm not quite sure where, but he's been there a long time. Joanie goes to see him occasionally, but there's not much money and the train trip is expensive so she doesn't go very often.

Another reason we stick together is because Billy is an albino. That means he's deficient in pigmentation or to put it more simply – he has pale skin, white hair, and pinkish eyes, a little like a white rabbit or one of those rats used for experiments. Tab and I have red curly hair and masses of freckles. She has thick glasses, but my eyes are fine.

Toby is what you'd call my best friend. He's huge. And I don't just mean overweight – he's big! And he's also uncoordinated, like his head is too far away from his feet to know what they are doing. Some people are frightened by his size, but really he's just a great big cuddly bear who wouldn't hurt a fly.

And last, but certainly not least, there's

Reggie. Actually, to be perfectly correct, his name's Arthur Reginald Forrester Upton-Middlesworth III. And I think that really says it all. Reggie was destined to be picked on from the moment he was named. He's small and quite sickly so he's missed a lot of school. He's also not allowed to take part in any sports and his mother is always fussing over him. She drops him off at school and picks him up every day from the gate. Anybody would think Reggie was five and not thirteen years old.

Anyway, that's our gang. And we've stayed together for mutual support, because one way or another, we're always getting picked on and called names. We pretty much keep to ourselves and try to stay out of trouble, but it's more difficult than you'd think. Billy has a hot temper and is always getting into fights over something or another. I'm forever having to bail him out. That's me, Max, the fixer of all things.

We've got a hangout down by the river. We're usually safe there as no one ever comes down. It could have something to do with the fact that it's behind the town dump – but we like it. And with the wind blowing the right way you can hardly smell the dump at all. Plus there're lots of cool things there. You wouldn't believe some of the stuff people throw out. We've managed to build a great clubhouse with things we've found. We've got to keep an eye out for old Joe, the guard. He knows we're there but pretends not to see us. We don't want to get him into trouble, though.

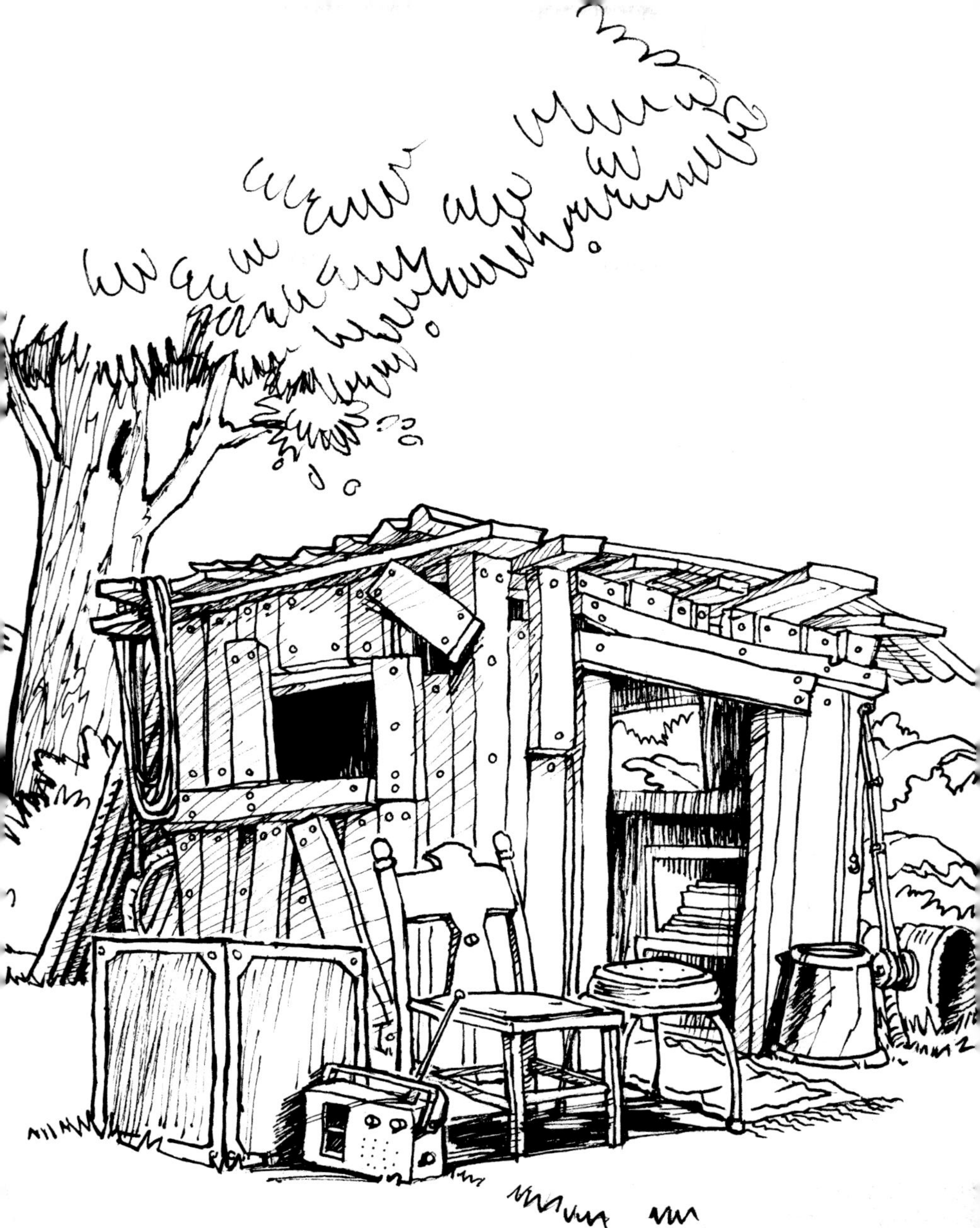

Today started out like any other ordinary Saturday, except it was miserable. It'd been raining for days. We'd all drifted down to the clubhouse. Reggie was last, as usual. He always had to tell his mother he was going to the library and then wait till she left to join us. His mother would have a fit if she knew he was hanging out down by the river – all those germs from the dump, not to mention his hanging out with the Bunton kids. He'd never be let out of the house again.

I was sitting there quietly reading a book, Toby and Tab were squabbling over Toby's chocolate, Billy was composing yet another song – he was set on a being a songwriter and he wasn't too bad at it – and Reggie had just finished poking around down at the river and was reading a comic book. He had a strange fascination for the river, considering he'd never been swimming in his life. The closest he'd ever got to it was sitting in a deep bathtub. It was all peaceful and normal,

well, as normal as we'd ever get, when I heard something out of the ordinary. My hearing was finely tuned because I was always on the lookout for trouble, not that I ever went looking for it as enough trouble came and found us.

"Quiet," I whispered to the others.

Immediately there was silence from the others as they tensed and looked around at me. They hadn't heard anything.

But there it was again, the distant sound of twigs breaking. Someone or something was definitely creeping up to the clubhouse.

I motioned for the others to move closer to me. I wondered who it could be. No one ever came down here. Just then I saw a movement in the trees and out sprang Jed, Cam, Ben, and Tom – trouble with a capital T. These boys were forever picking on us. They were the reason, half the time, that Billy lost his temper. There's only so much you can take and he wasn't old enough to shrug it off yet and not let it bother him.

"Well, look who we have here, Fatty, Skinny, and the Bunton kids," snarled a snooty voice.

It was Jed, self-confessed leader of the uptown snobs. It seemed they had nothing better to do on a Saturday than come and bother us.

The others all snickered. Cam picked up a stone and casually tossed it at the clubhouse. He was trying to tempt us into a fight.

"No fighting," I mouthed to the others, but I meant it especially for Billy. He sent me a look that told me he totally disagreed with me but did as I said. He was a good kid. He just had trouble controlling his temper.

Cam tossed another stone our way. It missed again but not by much. Ben sidled in closer. Unfortunately, he didn't look where he was going and fell, hitting his head on a protruding rock!

"Run," I yelled, taking advantage of Ben's misfortune to escape. "To the caves, quick."

We were all off and running while the others dealt with Ben. I could hear their yells all the way to the caves' entrance. This was bad. They'd come after us for sure now. And no one – but no one – would believe it was an accident and that it was all the uptown snobs' own fault.

# Into the Caves

The caves were only a short way away but Toby was already struggling to keep up. The rest of us got there way before him.

"Inside," I yelled, "quick!"

Tab looked up at me uncertainly. I nodded my head at her.

"We have no choice," I said. "Now go."

The others didn't look too pleased, either. But they filed inside the cave entrance, puffing and panting, and shrugging off the rain.

It's silly really but the caves are supposed to be haunted. The story goes that two kids wandered in there well over 50 years ago and no one ever saw either of them again.

The caves are a rabbit warren of disused mines

and naturally formed caverns and are absolutely off limits to everyone. I'm not totally convinced that the adults didn't make up the story to keep us out of the caves but even if they did, it works. No one I know had ever come near them. I mean, who'd want to anyway? Until now of course.

I waited outside for Toby and then followed him inside. The others were huddled together, looking more than a little scared. Reggie had managed to produce a flashlight from deep inside his jacket somewhere.

"My mother doesn't let me go out without it," he muttered, looking a little bashful, "in case of a power failure."

It is a little excessive, some of the stuff his mother makes him take with him every time he leaves the house. But over the next few hours I'd learn to be glad of it.

Reggie handed me the flashlight just as I heard the uptown snobs yelling from outside. They sounded mad.

"Come on, follow me," I whispered and took off down the passageway.

We twisted and turned our way through the tunnel for about ten minutes before I told everyone to stop. It was hard work. With only one flashlight for the five of us, it was pretty dark, and the floor wasn't exactly even. I figured we'd gone far enough into the caves that the others wouldn't follow us.

It was only then that I realized Tab was missing. We'd just made the first of many mistakes we would make that day. Each of us hadn't kept the person in front in sight.

"Where's Tab?" I demanded of the others, although I knew full well what a stupid question that was. If they knew where she was, she wouldn't be missing now, would she? I just felt like passing on some responsibility for once. They were all looking at me expectantly as though I'd use magic to make her reappear.

Everyone started talking at once.

"She was right behind me," spluttered Toby, trying to regain his breath.

"I thought she was in front of me," muttered Reggie sullenly.

"Right, I'll go back and get her," said Billy. "She can't be too far off."

But I grabbed the back of his shirt as he started back down the passageway. I wasn't about to let someone else disappear.

"Don't be silly," I said. "That's what got us into this mess to start with. We've got to stick together. Now, everyone count off. I'll start. One," I said.

"Two," that was Billy.

"Three," Reggie.

"Four," Toby.

"I'll lead the way," I said. "When I shout "one", I want you to all follow with your numbers. Keep the person in front in sight at all times. Apart from that, I want complete and utter silence. OK?"

I looked around at them all and they nodded in agreement, so I started walking back down the passage, listening all the time for any noises from up ahead.

# Trapped

Walking slowly back, I started to get a little worried. There were tunnels leading off from this main tunnel all the way along. I hadn't noticed them on the way in. We'd been running and not paying too much attention, but now, I realized, Tab could have wandered off into any of them. I started to get a horrible feeling in the pit of my stomach.

At every tunnel entrance, I made the others wait while I walked in ten steps and called out Tab's name. So far I'd heard nothing. But at the sixth tunnel I thought I heard something. I stopped and listened hard.

"Tab," I called out again.

"Max, I'm in here," came a voice.

It was Tab! I grabbed the others and we started down the tunnel.

"Just stay where you are," I called out. "Don't move. We're coming."

We found Tab a little way down the tunnel. Her backpack was trapped under a rock and in her efforts to free herself she'd twisted her shoulder straps in such a way that she couldn't move at all.

If she hadn't looked so forlorn I would have smiled. That backpack was a disaster. But it was her pride and joy. It used to be in the shape of a teddy bear but it was so old now that it was hard to tell what it was. It only had one eye left and the fur was rubbed off in patches. But Tab still loved it and carried it everywhere.

She had tripped and fallen trying to follow us down the passageway and by the time she'd stood up, we'd gone. She had heard the boys coming up behind us so she'd crawled down the tunnel to get away to safety. Unfortunately, without the flashlight it was pitch black and crawling along on her hands and knees she'd snagged her backpack on the rock and was now trapped. The good news was that she had heard the boys follow us down the passage and then give up and leave again. At least we now knew that they weren't still following us. We'd probably have to hide out for a few more hours but at least we were safe.

So now all I had to do was free Tab and we were home free. Fortunately Reggie had a Swiss Army knife so I had something to cut through the straps with.

"You'd be amazed how handy it is," Reggie had shrugged as he handed it over. It was just one more thing he produced that day that came in useful.

"You can't cut Mr. Bear!" shrieked Tab as I advanced with the knife. "Please, can't you just try to shift this rock?"

I looked at the others and Toby shrugged.

"No harm in trying," he said.

We all gathered around the rock, peering around the sides to see how it could be done. At this point I should have just ignored Tab's shrieks and cut Mr. Bear, but these things are easy to see in hindsight. The rock looked easy enough to move – big, yes, but Toby and I shouldn't have too much trouble, and Tab loved that backpack so much.

We fashioned a lever from a flat rock we found. Toby and I made the others stand back as we heaved and heaved until there was enough room for Tab to wriggle free. Once she was well clear, we let the rock back down with a thud.

And that's when the real problems began. The crash from the rock that reverberated around the passageway was deafening. Cracks started forming in the rock walls and smaller pieces of rock began to fall from the walls and ceilings. That's when we heard the rumbling noises start. And for the second time that day I screamed out,

"Run!"

In only a matter of seconds, the cave started to disintegrate around us. It must have been totally unstable to begin with. We ran and ran down that tunnel until, after what seemed like an eternity, the rumbling stopped. It was only then that I dared to look around. The passage back was blocked. We were trapped. The only good part was that in the mad dash down into the caves we hadn't lost anybody. We were all present and accounted for, just trapped in a dark stuffy cave, and no one except the uptown snobs knew where we might be – as if they'd care! Things were not looking good.

# Riding the Rapids

Everybody looked scared. Tab was shaking like a leaf. Yet again everybody was looking to me for a solution. Billy started to tear at the rocks with his hands, trying to burrow us a passage back through. He hated being in confined spaces and I could relate to that. I pulled him off.

"Stop that," I said. "We're trapped! There's no way through there. That rock's too unstable for us to try anything. There's only one way out of here now and that's down this passage."

They all looked at me like I was mad. Go even deeper into the caves? There was no telling what we'd meet up ahead and we had no idea if the tunnel even went anywhere. But as far as I could see, it was the only option left to us and seeing as

I was in charge, I was making the decisions. But first things first, we had to get a little more organized. I had no idea how long we'd been down here now and all this frantic running here and there had done nothing but get us into more trouble. We had to be a lot more responsible, and, as usual, it would be up to me to sort it out.

I ordered everybody to empty their pockets. You wouldn't believe some of the stuff Reggie pulled out. Some of it came in quite handy later on, though. And between Tab and Toby we had enough food to last us a while, that was if I took charge of it and rationed it. With much grumbling, they handed over all their food and I rationed out a portion to each of us. Once we had a little food in our stomachs, I explained the numbering system to Tab. We all counted off again, then set off down the tunnel in search of a way out.

Not far down the tunnel my finely tuned hearing picked up some unusual gurgling noises.

I told everyone to stop while I listened. It definitely sounded like running water. About five minutes later, we came across the gurgling sound again, only much louder now. A river was rushing across our path, and not just a little river, a full raging torrent of a river.

This was bad. This was very bad. The river was running straight across our path – fast. There was a drop from where we stood down to the river and I could see our tunnel continuing on the other side. It was too wide to jump across. There was only one thing to do. One of us would have to swim. And that would be me.

Luckily Reggie's pockets had turned up a ball of thick nylon twine and I was beginning to come up with a plan. I tied one end of the twine around my waist and the other end around the others with Toby as the anchor. That way if I didn't make it to the other side, Toby could help the others pull me back. And if I did make it, then they could cross the river holding on to the twine. The plan sounded good at the time and the others agreed.

I gingerly lowered myself down the drop until my feet hit the water. Boy, was it cold! In fact, not just cold but icy right-through-to-the-bones cold. Luckily it wasn't too deep. My feet hit the bottom just as the water hit my kneecaps. I felt the pull of the current as soon as I let go of the side. I took a few deep breaths and then pushed my way out into the middle. The going was slow as there was a myriad of rocks underfoot trying to trip me and the current was forever pulling at me, but after what seemed like an eternity, I made it to the other side.

The others cheered when I lifted myself up onto the dry ground.

"One down, four to go," I muttered to myself under my breath.

We'd decided on the order we'd cross before I went across and it was Billy next. Being the daredevil that he was, he crossed much faster than I had and was looking quite pleased with himself when he made it to my side of the river.

Reggie was next and seemed nervous. It wasn't surprising since he'd never swam before and was now going to tackle a raging river. To his credit, though, he didn't whine about it. He just carefully lowered himself down the way I had and set off. Trouble hit when he got about halfway across. Billy was on his stomach leaning out from the bank and holding out his hand to grab Reggie when he got close enough. Reggie saw Billy's hand, panicked, and made a wild grab for it. Reggie lost his footing and was swiftly picked up by the current and dragged downstream. Billy was taken by surprise and without having a good grip on anything was quickly dragged into the water after Reggie. Tab, still over the other side of the stream, didn't have much of a chance and was quickly dragged in as well. Their combined weight and the pull of the current was too much for Toby and I and we soon followed them into the river. It all happened so quickly I could barely believe what was happening. The flaw in my great plan struck me right then. Although tying us all together had seemed like a good idea, it also meant that we'd all get dragged in together if anyone slipped up.

I gave myself up to the pull of the river and let myself be dragged along. After what seemed like an eternity, but what was probably only about 30 seconds, I felt the current lessen. Gasping for breath, I raised my head and tried to have a look around. Although it was still dark, it wasn't quite as pitch black as it had been and I could make out a few things here and there. I dragged myself over to the water's edge and hauled myself out of the water, screaming out the others' names the whole time. Somewhere during my rapid ride, the string around my waist had come untied and I had no idea where the others were now.

Slowly, out of the gloom they appeared. They all looked a little worse for wear but in one piece which was the important part. Even in the dark I could see that Reggie was green. It didn't look like he'd enjoyed his first swim at all.

After the rush of relief at finding that we were all present and accounted for, I began to take stock of what we had left. All our food and supplies were gone and we were wet and cold. We had plenty of water now, which was a positive but it didn't seem like much in the light of what we'd lost.

So, there we were, cold, wet, hungry, and lost. Did I mention petrified? And trapped? And everyone was looking to me for a plan.

# Ghost Attack

I took a quick walk around the space we were in. It seemed like we were trapped in a very large cavern. Although it was quite a large space and very dark without the flashlight, it only took me about ten minutes to scout around. The walls of the cavern were too smooth to climb and offered up no tunnels.

There was something gnawing at the back of my mind, something that I thought would help us, but for the time being I couldn't bring the thought to life.

I returned to the rest of them with a glum look on my face. It looked like the only way out was back in the river. I for one was not eager to take the plunge again just yet.

The gloomy expressions on the faces of the others reflected my own. No one wanted to go back in the icy water. We were still wet from our last swim and the cold was starting to seep into our bones and there was no guarantee that it would work out anyway. We huddled in a group trying to keep warm while we discussed our options. There weren't many.

However, Reggie, for one, was adamant that he was not going back in the river. I couldn't really blame him. He still looked terrified from the last dip. But it was looking like our only choice. Once again I had the feeling that there was something I was missing.

Right then, I heard a rustling noise coming from far up above. I hushed the others as I strained to listen. The rustling noise got louder and louder until we could see a mass of black shapes swirling above us.

"It's the ghosts," shrieked Tab, as she erupted into a fit of screams, making everyone panic.

Suddenly the thought that was at the back of my mind became clear and I started to laugh. I just couldn't stop.

Slowly the rustling noise stopped and the black shapes swirled away. Tab stopped screaming and the others all calmed down and looked at me in amazement to see why I was laughing. No one could see anything even slightly amusing in the situation, and I couldn't blame them.

"What is so funny?" demanded Toby.

I couldn't answer him for a moment as I was still laughing too hard.

"Don't you see?" I eventually managed to splutter through my giggles.

"See what?" Billy demanded, looking more than a little bewildered and suspicious at my unaccustomed outbreak.

"'See'. Exactly that, 'see'. I can see your faces. It's still dark but not as dark as it has been," I told them gleefully. That was the thought that had been gnawing at the back of my mind.

It was gloomy in the cave but not pitch black like it had been. And the bats had made me realize that. For, of course, they were bats we had just disturbed and not the ghosts Tab had proclaimed.

"There's got to be a light source somewhere and the bats we just saw have to exit the cavern at some point. We've just got to find the opening and we're saved," I said excitedly.

The sudden change in the group with that little speech was amazing. Smiles came back on their faces and everyone started talking at once. Now all we needed was a plan.

While the others had been panicking over the "ghosts," I'd carefully watched the bats to see where they were exiting.

It looked like there was a tunnel about halfway up the cavern wall on the far side from where we were sitting.

I was pretty sure that once we got up there, the tunnel would lead us to the exit hole and

freedom. How we would get up there was another story.

# The Tunnel

We peered up into the darkness, straining our eyes to try and see the tunnel entrance. It definitely looked like there was something up there, but it was hard to tell in the gloom. Once again I took control.

"Well, there's nothing else to do," I said. "I'm going up. If there is a tunnel up there, I'll follow it out and go to find help. The rest of you sit tight here and don't move. You'll be fine." Once again, I was speaking with more confidence than I actually felt.

The others looked a little apprehensive, but they knew as well as I did that it was our only possible way out of the gloomy trap we were in.

Toby gave me a push up to start me off and I

struggled to find some footholds in the smooth cliff wall. Luckily, the walls of the cavern became uneven a little way up and provided quite a few handholds for me to grab onto. This was quite puzzling, but as I could reach the first handhold standing on Toby's shoulders, I didn't think much of it at the time, just started to climb.

It was the scariest five minutes of my life. I eventually made it up to the tunnel entrance and pulled myself up onto the ledge. I was just congratulating myself on a job well done when there was a loud scream from down below. I could recognize Tab's scream anywhere.

I crawled out over the edge on my stomach and looked down at the others.

At first I couldn't make out anything at all in the dim light, then I thought I could make out their shadowy shapes. It looked like they were standing in water. I rubbed my eyes.

"What's going on?" I yelled down.

"It's the river," Toby yelled back. "It's broken

its banks and is starting to flood the cavern. It's up to our knees already. We can't wait for you. We'll have to come up, too."

"That explains the state of the cliff wall," I thought to myself. "It must be raining outside and the runoff is causing the river to swell and flood. It must happen every time it rains and over time the floodwaters have worn the cavern walls smooth."

My problem now was how to get the others up to the ledge. We'd lost all our twine in the river ride and I was positive Reggie and Tab wouldn't make it up the cliff.

"Take off your T-shirts!" I yelled down to them. "Tie them together and throw them up to me. We'll use them as a rope to haul you up."

They quickly did as I ordered. I tied one end of the "rope" around my middle to anchor it and threw the other end down.

"Tie the end around your middle and I'll haul you up. You first, Billy!" I shouted. I had to get someone up to the ledge to help me with the others and if I knew Billy as well as I thought I did, he wouldn't let me just haul him up, he'd try and climb so there wouldn't be much strain on me. And I was dead right, for the next minute Billy's head popped up on the ledge and with a grin he was next to me. He untied himself and threw the end back down to the others.

"Piece of cake," he grinned smugly as he took up position behind me.

Tab was next. Billy and I easily pulled her up onto the ledge. Reggie was the same. Last was Toby. This would be hard but not impossible I told myself.

By this time, Toby was practically swimming. The water was swirling around his chest but he had valiantly lifted the others up, standing his ground in the rushing waters, and we weren't about to leave him there.

We threw the "rope" down for the last time and Toby tied it around his middle.

"You're going to have to help us and try to climb!" I yelled down.

The swirling waters had now lifted Toby off his feet but with the rope anchoring him to us he wasn't drifting away. A semi-plan was starting to form in my mind.

"How are you doing down there?" I yelled down at Toby.

"OK," came back the reply. "It's pretty cold but I'm just floating here next to the cliff. I'm certainly not going anywhere."

"Wait until the water rises enough for you to get some handholds!" I yelled back down. "Then start climbing. We'll be holding on to the rope from up here so don't worry, you won't fall. Just take it slowly."

Toby yelled back his agreement. Then we waited another few minutes until we heard his voice again.

"OK, I've got a handhold and I'm coming up!" he yelled.

I was a little uneasy as to whether we'd actually be able to hold him if he did fall. I could imagine his weight pulling us all over. But I was hoping the fact that Toby would think we'd be able to catch him would give him enough confidence not to fall – mind over matter, so to speak.

It was a heart-stopping few minutes as we carefully braced ourselves and took up the slack. Finally, after what seemed like forever, we saw Toby's fingers appear on the ledge. I hadn't realized I'd been holding my breath until it all came out in a rush. Toby looked extremely pleased – wet, but pleased nonetheless. He wasn't usually the athletic type but what with all the running and climbing and swimming he'd done today, he was starting to change his mind.

We all stood chattering on the ledge for a few more minutes, sorting out our T-shirts and getting dressed again before we set off. We were all eager to be out of the cave and warm and dry again.

We didn't stop to think that there might not be a way out, that we might be trapped down in the cave forever.

The tunnel we were now in sloped gently up. We started walking, full of high hopes that we would soon be home again. Billy even started singing a part of one of his new songs as we made our way slowly up the tunnel.

But, gradually, the walk got steeper and steeper and the tunnel narrowed until we were practically crawling along. I was worried that Toby would get stuck, then we'd be in real trouble. I could only hope that the passageway didn't get any narrower.

On the positive side, it was definitely getting much lighter. In fact, it wasn't long before I was

almost certain I could see a tiny opening at the end of the tunnel.

"I can see the opening!" I yelled back to the others excitedly when I spotted the pinprick of light at the end of the tunnel.

We stepped up the pace again, as much as we could in the narrow tunnel, and the next minute we had all crawled out of the tunnel and into the fresh air again.

There were whoops of laughter all round as we eagerly breathed the fresh air and stretched our legs. It was still raining but since we were all wet already anyway, it didn't matter. We ran around like mad things.

It was over! We had entered the caves, even been trapped inside them, and still lived to tell the story. And what a story it was! I was already thinking about writing the whole thing down so we'd never ever forget.

"I've got to go," Reggie finally said. "My mother's picking me up from the library and she'll worry if I'm not there."